# The Fun of Getting Thin

*Samuel G. Blythe*

# Contents

# THE FUN OF GETTING THIN

## BY
## Samuel G. Blythe

# CHAPTER I
# FAT

A fat man is a joke; and a fat woman is two jokes--one on herself and the other on her husband. Half the comedy in the world is predicated on the paunch. At that, the human race is divided into but two classes--fat people who are trying to get thin and thin people who are trying to get fat.

Fat, the doctors say, is fatal. I move to amend by striking out the last two letters of the indictment. Fat is fat. It isn't any more fatal to be reasonably fat than to be reasonably thin, but it's a darned sight more uncomfortable. So far as being unreasonably thin or unreasonably fat is concerned, I suppose the thin person has the long end of it. I never was thin, so I don't know. However,

I have been fat--notice that "have been"? And if there is any phase of human enjoyment, any part of life, any occupation, avocation, divertisement, pleasure or pain where the fat man has the better of it in any regard, I failed to discover it in the twenty years during which I looked like the rear end of a hack and had all the bodily characteristics of a bale of hay.

When you come to examine into the actuating motives for any line of human endeavor you will find that vanity figures about ninety per cent, directly or indirectly, in the assay. The personal equation is the ruling equation. Women want to be thinner because they will look better--and so do men. Likewise, women want to be plumper because they will look better--and so do men. This holds up to forty years. After that it doesn't make much difference whether either men or women look any better than they have been looking, so far as the great end and aim of all life is concerned. Consequently fat men and fat women after forty want to be thinner for reasons of health and comfort, or quit and resign themselves to their further years of obesity.

Now I am over forty. Hence my experiments in reduction may be taken at this time as grounded on a desire for comfort--not that I did not make many campaigns against my fat before I was forty. I fought it now and then, but always retreated before I won a victory. This time, instead of skirmishing valiantly for a space and then being ignominiously and fatly routed by the powerful forces of food and drink, I hung stolidly to the line of my original attack, harassed the enemy by a constant and deadly fire--and one morning discovered I had the foe on the run.

It always makes me laugh to hear people talk about losing flesh--unless, of course, the decrease in weight is due to illness. No healthy person, predisposed to fat, ever lost any flesh. If that person gets rid of any weight, or girth, or fat, it isn't lost--it is fought off, beaten off. The victim struggles with it, goes to the mat with it, and does not debonairly drop it. He eliminates it with stern effort and much travail of the spirit. It is a job of work, a grueling combat to the finish, a task that appalls and usually repels.

The theory of taking off fat is the simplest theory in the world. It is announced, in four words: Stop eating and drinking. The practice of fat reduction is the most difficult thing in the world. Its difficulties are comprehended in two words: You cannot. The flesh is willing, but the spirit is weak. The success of the undertaking lies in the triumph of the will over the appetite. There's a lovely line of cant for you! Triumph of the will over the appetite. It sounds like the preaching of a professional food faddist, who tells the people they eat too much and then slips away and wolfs down four pounds of beefsteak at a sitting. However, I suppose it is necessary to say this once in a dissertation like this--and it is said.

In writing about this successful experiment of mine in reducing weight I have no theories to advance except one, and no instructions to give. I don't know whether my method would take an ounce off any other person in the world, and I don't care. I only know it took more than fifty pounds off me. I am not advancing any argument, medicinal or otherwise, for my plan. I never talked to a doctor about it, and never shall. If there are fat men and fat women who are fat for the same reasons I was fat I suppose they can get thin the way I got thin.

If they are fat for other reasons I suppose they cannot. I don't know about either proposition.

I have great respect for doctors--so much respect, in fact, that I keep diligently away from them. I know the preliminaries of their game and can take a dose of medicine myself as skillfully as they can administer it. Also, I know when I have a fever, and have a working knowledge of how my heart should beat and my other bodily functions be performed. I have frequently found that a prescription, unintelligibly written but looking very wise, is highly efficacious when folded carefully and put in the pocketbook instead of being deposited with a druggist. I suppose that comes from a sort of hereditary faith in amulets. No doubt the method would be even more efficacious if the prescription were tied on a string and hung around the neck. I shall try that some time when my wife lugs in a doctor on me.

Still, doctors are interesting as a class. After you get beyond the let-me-feel-your-pulse-and-see-your-tongue preliminaries they are versatile and ingenious. Almost always, after you tell them what is the matter with you, they will know--not every time, but frequently. Also, they will take any sort of a chance with you in the interest of science. However, they generally send out for a specialist when they are ill themselves. When you come to think of it that is but natural. Almost any man, whether professional or not, will take a chance with somebody else that he wouldn't quite go through with on himself. Besides, doctors treat comparative strangers for the most part, and the interests of science are to be conserved.

Almost any doctor can tell you how to get thin. To be sure, no doctor will tell you to do the same things any other doctor prescribes, but it all simmers down to the same thing: Cut out the starchy foods and sweets, and take exercise. Also: Don't drink alcohol. The variations that can be played on this simple theme by a skillful doctor are endless. When a real specialist in fat reduction gets hold of you--a real, earnest reducer--he can contrive a diet that would make a living skeleton thin--and likewise put him in his little grave. I have had diets handed to me that would starve a humming-bird, and diets that would put flesh on a bronze statue; and all to the same end--reduction. Science has been monkeying with nourishment for the past ten or fifteen years to the exclusion of many other branches of research; and about all that has happened to the nourishment is the large elimination of nutriment from it.

# CHAPTER II
# THE SO-CALLED CURES

Broadly speaking, the methods of fat reduction most in vogue are divided into four classes-- mechanical, physical, medicinal and dietary. The first two are not worth considering by a man who has anything else to do. I do not doubt that a man who could devote his whole time to the work could, by means of some of the appliances offered-- from the apparatus in a gymnasium to rubber shirts, get off fat--nor do I doubt the efficacy of exercise and its accompaniments in the way of sweating and baths and all that; but when a person has a living to make these methods are useless, not through any demerit of their own but because the man who is fat hasn't the time or opportunity and, more than all, soon fails in the inclination to use them.

If you can tell me anything more ghastly than taking a system of canned exercises in the morning or at night in one's bedroom or bathroom, or elsewhere, with no other incentive than some physical gain that, when you come to sum it up, is largely fictitious in value--or comes inevitably to be thought so--I would like to have you step forward and name it. I have been all through that phase of it, and I know; and I also know by heart the patter of the persons who recommend it. Further, I know the person round the forties doesn't live who enjoys this sort of thing--no matter what he says about it; and without enjoyment exercise is of no use or worse than useless. It can be done, of course; and lumps of muscle can be stuck on almost any part of the body-- but what's the use to the person who has to make a living? Then, too, I am speaking now of methods that can be used by men and women who are no longer young. A young man can and will do stunts in physical culture that an older man cannot do, either satisfactorily or comfortably.

So far as the medicinal or drug method of fat reduction is concerned, any fat man or woman who takes drugs to reduce flesh, or to help, deserves all that he or she will get--and that will be plenty. There's no need of saying anything further on that subject. Then there remains the dietary method--the old familiar friend, diet. Starting with William Banting--maybe it didn't start with William, but before him--but, starting with Bill for present purposes, there have been more systems of diet invented and promulgated than there have been systems of religion--and that means about one in every hundred has evolved a system.

You can get them of all sorts and all sure to do the work, ranging from an exclusive diet of beefsteak and spinach to desiccated hay and creamed alfalfa. There are monodiets, duodiets, vegetable diets, fruit diets, nut diets--all kinds of diets--each guaranteed to take off flesh if you have too much or to put it on if you have too little. Basically, however, the antiflesh diets are about the same. You are told to cut out everything you want to eat and exist on triply toasted bread and the white meat of a chicken, or string beans and sawdust, or any other combination the sharps say will not produce fat, but will sustain life in a lingering form. They surround these diet talks and presentments with a lot of frills about proteins and calories and all that sort of guff, and make it as difficult as possible. Now, mark you, I am not saying diet--scientific diet--is not a good thing, a magnificent step forward in the progress of this world; but I am saying that the average fat-reducing diet is impossible to any but a man or woman of the ultimate will-power, and is a hardship that need not be endured. I have tried these diets, and I know! They may help reduce flesh, but they are not easy to follow and they do not contain things that any person wants to eat or is accustomed to eat, or will eat, to the exclusion of things that person does want to eat and will eat. It can be done. One of these diets can be followed if the will-power is there, and the flesh will come off; but the method does not conduce to the best results--the physical force is reduced, and there is a much easier way.

I have one of these diet lists before me now from the highest-priced flesh-reducing specialist in the world, who claims to have taken mountains of flesh off mountainous men. In the beginning, for example, it says:

"You will understand, of course, that sugar is entirely debarred.  Also, that fats, milk, cheese, cream, eggs, and so on, are cut off for the time being.  Also that bread and farinaceous foods are all cut off.  In place of bread or toast you must use gluten biscuits." For breakfast, in this dietary, one or two gluten biscuits are allowed and a cup of unsweetened coffee.  Also, six ounces of lean grilled steak, chops or chicken, and any white fish--or the whites of two eggs.

This is about the layout for luncheon and dinner. It is all about as exciting and appetizing as that.  The proposition is, of course, that you are not taking food which will make fat and you must, therefore, inevitably lose flesh.  So far so good; but the difficulty is not in the system, but in the hardship of carrying it out.  You can't have anything to eat that you want to eat.  You torture yourself for a space and lose some flesh; then when you do go back to your normal method of eating the flesh comes galloping back--and there you are!  It is the same with exercise.  You can take off fat by exercise; but, once you begin, you are doomed to everlasting exercise, for the minute you stop back comes the fat--and more of it than you had before you began to reduce.

It is a tough game, anyway you play it, if you are disposed to be fat. No man living, who isn't a freak, can persist always in one diet. Nor can any man who has anything else on his mind be always exercising--especially after he has reached forty years of age, when there are so many better things to do and time is valuable, and the real idea of how to live has just begun to percolate. Also, until one is forty, if reasonably healthy, flesh is a joke, and not so much of a burden as it becomes later. I haven't a thing in the world against any or all of these methods. I have tried most of them and know most of them are bogus; but I am not trying to dissuade any person from taking off fat in any way that suits any individual fancy or the fancy of any reducer into whose hands the victim may have fallen. If you have a good method go to it--and more power to you!

My idea is this: I am setting down here a record of my own experiences, and that is all. Every person who does not like what I have to say is cheerfully advised to lump it. Any person who is as fat as I was and who wants to get thinner is at liberty to follow my method.

If circumstances are similar results will be similar. If not there will be no results. I am not advising or urging or putting forth any propaganda. Here is what happened. It may suit you or it may not. Either way I am indifferent. In the words of the coon song: "I've got mine!"

I hope I make myself clear. I have no mission or message or any flubdub of that kind. I am not one of those boys who urge you to do this for your own good. I have read a ton of literature put out by persons who found something that agreed with them and immediately started out to reform the world along that line. Your reformer, anyhow, is a person who wants all the rest of the world to do as he wants the rest of the world to do, not as the rest of the world wants to do. And the reason reformers get past so numerously is because our society is so constituted that we spend every one of our brief years doing what other people want us to do and tell us to do, and never do anything we ourselves want to do. Once I got seventeen pounds of books telling that the only way to cure everything was to fast. I knew a man who tried that. The results were grand. He fasted a long time and cured himself of what ailed him. Only, unfortunately, just before the last vestige of disease was removed the fasting killed him. I contend that man might just as well have died of what ailed him originally as to cure that disease and die of the cure. It seems to me it is as broad as it is long.

However, have at this fat-reduction process of mine! You must bear with a few personal reminiscences. I was a big, husky brute of a boy--thick-chested, broad-shouldered, country-bred and with an appetite that knew no bounds. After I got going at my business, when I was twenty-five or so, I was pinned down to a desk for about ten years. I worked hard in a most exacting place. I was so healthy it hurt. I had just as much appetite for food as I had ever had; but I didn't get a chance to bat around as I had been accustomed to do and burn up that food. The result was inevitable. I began to get fat. I had a big chest--forty-six inches--and the fat filled in underneath. That big chest, combined with my broad shoulders, concealed the size of my paunch, and I didn't realize I was accumulating that paunch until it was soldered, riveted, lashed, glued, nailed and otherwise fastened to me.

When I got my growth I weighed about one hundred and eighty-five pounds and was a pretty formidable physical proposition. When I woke up to the fact that I was getting fat I found I weighed two hundred and twenty pounds. That extra thirty-five pounds was mostly fat--excess baggage. Still, it didn't bother me any. I had the strength to tote it round and had the shoulders and the chest to conceal it. I didn't show any bay window, as most fat men do. As they used to say: "You're big all over. You carry it all right."

All this time I was eating three or four times a day and eating everything that came my way. Also, I drank some--not excessively, but some whisky and some beer, and occasionally some wine and cocktails--about the average amount of drinking the average man does. I thought I was getting too fat, and I wrestled with a bicycle all one summer, taking long rides and plugging round a good deal. I did some centuries, but continued eating like a horse--naturally because of the outdoor exercise--and drank a good deal of beer. As will be seen, all the fat I had was legitimate enough. I put it on myself. There was no hereditary nonsense about it. I was responsible for every ounce of it. The net result of that summer's bicycle campaign was a gain of five pounds in weight. I was harder--but I was fatter, too.

When I was thirty-five I began to experiment. I then weighed two hundred and twenty-five pounds. I went to the canned-exercise, the physical-torture professor, the diet, the salts, and all the rest of it, taking off a few pounds but putting it all back again--and more--as soon as I stopped.

These attempts numbered about two a year. Between times I ate as I wanted to and drank as I pleased. Things ran along until the first of January, 1911. I knew I was getting fatter, for my tailor told me so and my belts and old clothes all proved it. Still, I didn't bother much. I thought I was lingering round about two hundred and thirty-five--too much, of course; but I got away with it pretty well, except in hot weather and when I went up in the high mountains, and I was reasonably content. I was fat, all right. My waist was only two inches smaller than my chest and that meant my waist was forty-four inches in girth. As a matter of fact, being scant five feet ten and a half, I was bigger than a house; but I deluded myself with that stuff about my broad shoulders and my deep chest, and thought it didn't show. It did show, of course. I was a fat man--a big fat man--carrying forty pounds or more of excess weight.

I had dieted and quit; exercised and quit; gone on the waterwagon and fallen off; had fussed round a good deal, spending a lot of money in the attempt, and I was getting fatter all the time. I hated to admit that fact. I tried to fool myself into the conviction that I wasn't getting any larger--and all the time I knew I was. I even went so far as to stop getting on the scales; and when anybody--as almost everybody did--said, "Why, you're getting bigger, ain't you?" I always replied: "No, I think not. I stick along about two hundred and thirty-five pounds."

A year ago last summer I went up into the mountains, where I usually go for my fun. I had noticed a shortness of breath and a wheeziness in previous summers, and had felt my heart pounding pretty hard; but that summer I noticed these things acutely. I couldn't get any air to breathe. My heart pounded like a pneumatic riveter. Any little exercise tired me; and when in

the lowlands in hot weather I was the perspiring marvel and the most uncomfortable as well as the sloppiest
person you ever saw.  It was fierce!

I was doing a good deal of walking in those days--had
to burn up the fuel I was taking into my body.  Also, I
noticed it was mighty hard to keep awake after dinner
unless I got out into the air and kept moving. I felt well
enough and the doctors said I was organically all right.
I kept informed on those points--but I was fat!  Also,
though I lied to myself, I knew I was getting fatter.

## CHAPTER III
## FACING THE TISSUE

On New Year's Day, 1911, I weighed myself. I don't know why, for I hadn't been on a scale for two or three years. I set the weight at two hundred and thirty-five and it bounded up like a rubber ball; so I shoved it along to two hundred and forty and it still stayed up in the air. When I got a balance I found I weighed two hundred and forty-seven pounds. I was amazed! Also, I was scared; for it instantly occurred to me that if I had gone up to two hundred and forty-seven in two or three years from two hundred and thirty-five I should keep on going up if my manner of living didn't change--and that presently I should weigh three hundred!

That two hundred and forty-seven pounds was a fac-

er.  I was forced to admit to myself that I was fat, dis-
gustingly fat--too fat; and that I should get fatter!  So I
sat down and looked the situation in the eye.  I recount-
ed all my former efforts to get thin and discarded them
one by one.  I knew myself, and knew the ordinary diet
proposition and the ordinary exercise proposition were
not for me.  I knew I was wheezy and that my heart was
getting choked with fat; that there were great folds of
it on me, and that it was up to me to get rid of it or quit
and wait for the inevitable end.  If it kept on I knew I
should blow up some fine day. Besides, I was uric-acidy,
rheumatic and stertorous and clumsy.  I had about fifty
or sixty pounds of poisonous junk wrapped round me,
and I knew I should suffer for it in the end, though I
didn't feel it much and carried it with a fair assumption
of lightness.

I was not an amateur at the game.  I had been through
the mill.  I spent several days in going over the whole
matter.  It was reasonably simple, too, and needn't have
taken so much of my time; but I was protecting myself,
you see, gold-bricking myself--trying to find a way out
that would not deprive me of things I liked to do, of

pleasures I wanted to enjoy.  It was pure selfishness that dominated me and made me do so much figuring on a proposition I knew was contained in a sentence; but I did fight to hang on to the old way of living.

After each session of false logic and selfish hypothesis I invariably came back to the same proposition, which is the only proposition--and that was: What makes fat? Food and drink.  How can you reduce fat?  By reducing the amount of food and drink--that is all there is or was to it. The only way to get rid of the effects of overeating and overdrinking is to stop overeating and overdrinking.

I went over my food habit.  I was accustomed to eating a big hired-man's breakfast--fruit, coffee, eggs, waffles, hot bread, sausage, anything that came along; and I heaved in a lot of it--not a little--a lot!  I didn't eat so much at luncheon, but I ate plenty; and at night I simply cleaned up the table.  I wasn't so strong on sweets and pastry, because I usually drank a few highballs during the day, and highballs and cocktails and sweets do not go well together--that is, the man who takes alcohol into his system usually does not care for sweets.  Beer was one of my long suits too--Pilsner beer. I did like that!

I looked this food habit squarely in the face. I impaled the drink habit with my glittering eye. I knew I was eating about sixty per cent more than I needed or could use, and that I was drinking a hundred per cent more. I knew that nothing makes fat but food and drink. I knew excess of food will make any animal fat and I saw I had been eating freely of the most fattening kinds of food. I knew beer and liquor were made of grain, and that grain is used to fatten steers and cows and pigs. I refused to adopt a diet like any of those unpalatable ones I had experimented with, but the remedy was as plain as the cause. It was simple enough if I had the nerve to go through with it.

Inasmuch as an excess of food and drink make an excess of fat, it follows that the reduction in the amount of food will stop that fat-forming and give the body a chance to burn up the excess fat already formed. That was my conclusion. Mind you, I reached that conclusion before I made any of my arguments; but I didn't want to admit it as reasonable or logical, for I hated to give up the pleasures of the table and the sociability that came with the sort of drinking I did. I was trying to find a way out that would be easy and comfortable. And all the time I was getting fatter! The scales told me that.

This backing and filling and argument with myself lasted all through January and part of February. It took me six weeks to get myself into the frame of mind where I admitted the truth of my conclusion. I was no hero. I didn't want to do it. I loved it all too well. I was as rank a coward in the beginning as you ever saw! It appalled me to think of restricting myself in any way, for I liked the pleasures that I knew I must forego. However, when I got up to two hundred and fifty pounds I sat down and had it out with myself.

"Here!" I said to myself. "You big stuff, you now weigh two hundred and fifty pounds! In another year or two you will weigh two hundred and seventy-five pounds! You are uncomfortable and heavy on your feet, and you are gouty and wheezy; and it's a cinch you'll die in a few years if you keep on this way. You know all this fat is caused by an excess of food and drink, and you know it can be taken off by a reduction in those fatmakers. Are you going to stick round here so fat you are a joke, uncomfortable, miserable when it's hot, in your own way and in the way of everybody else, when, if you've got the will-power of a chickadee, you can get back to reasonable proportions and comfort merely by denying yourself things you do not need?"

All the old arguments obtruded. See what I should lose! Life would be a dull and dreary affair--a dun, dismal proposition. I admitted that. On the other hand, however, life would not be a wheezy, sweaty, choked-heart, uncomfortable proposition. I finally decided I would go to it. And I did.

My method may be utterly unscientific. I suppose it hasn't a scientific leg to stand on. Still, it did the business. And I maintain that results are what we are looking for. The end justifies the means. I didn't figure out a diet. I had a dozen of them at home that had cost me all the way from two dollars to two hundred and fifty dollars each. I didn't buy a system of exercise. I read no books and consulted no doctors. What I did was this: I cut down the amount of food I ate sixty per cent and I cut out alcohol altogether! I carried out my argument to its logical conclusion so far as it concerned myself. I didn't give a hoot whether it would help or hurt or concern any other person in the world. It was my body I was experimenting on, and I did what I dad-blamed pleased and asked no advice--nor took any.

Instead of a hot-bread--I have the greatest hot-bread artist in the world at my house, bar none!--waffle, sausage, kidney-stew, lamb-chop, fried-egg and so forth sort of breakfast, I cut that meal down to some fruit, a couple of pieces of dry, hard toast, two boiled eggs and coffee. I cut out the luncheon altogether. No more luncheon for me! I cut down my dinners to about forty per cent of what I had been eating. I diminished the quantity, but not the variety. I ate everything that came along, but I didn't eat so much or half so much. Instead of two slices of roast beef, for example, I ate only one small slice. Instead of two baked or browned potatoes, I ate only half of one. Instead of three or four slices of bread, I ate only one. I didn't deprive myself of a single thing I liked, but I cut the quantity away down. And I quit drinking alcohol absolutely.

What happened? This is what happened: Eating food

is just as much a habit as breathing or any other physical function. I had got myself into the habit of eating large quantities of food. Also, I had accustomed my system to certain amounts of alcohol. I was organized on that basis--fatly and flabbily organized, to be sure, but organized just the same. Now, then, when I arbitrarily cut down the amount of food and drink for which my system was organized that entire system rose up in active revolt and yelled for what it had been accustomed to get. There wasn't a minute for more than three months when I wasn't hungry, actually hungry for food; when the sight of food did not excite me and when I did not have a physical longing and appetite for food; when my stomach did not seem to demand it and my palate howl for it. It was different with the drinking. I got over that desire rather promptly, but with a struggle, at that; but the food-yearn was there for weeks and weeks, and it was a fight--a bitter, bitter fight!

When I went to the table and saw the good things on it, and knew I intended only to eat small portions of them, especially of my favorite desserts and my beloved hot-bread, I simply had to grip the sides of my chair

and use all the will-power I had to keep from reach-
ing out and grabbing something and stuffing it into my
mouth!  My friends used to think it was all a joke.  It
was farther from being a joke than anything you ever
heard about.  It was a tragedy--a grim, relentless trag-
edy!  It was acute physical suffering.  My body cried
out for that same amount of food I had been giving it
all those years.  I wanted to give it that same amount.  I
have had to leave the table time and time again to get
hold of myself and go back to the smaller portions I had
allotted to myself.  I liked to eat, you know.

Nothing much happened for a few weeks, though
the waistband of my trousers grew looser.  Then a lot
of excess baggage seemed to drop away all at once.  I
weighed myself and found I had taken off twenty-five
pounds.  Friends told me to quit--that I should overdo
it.  I laughed at them.  I knew I was still twenty-five
pounds too heavy and I was just getting into my stride.
It is strange how men, and especially fat men, who
haven't the nerve to reduce themselves, think a man
must be sick if he takes off flesh.  I knew I wasn't sick.
Indeed, I was just beginning to get well.

By the end of three months I had taken off thirty-five pounds. It was coming off well, too. My face wasn't haggard or wrinkled. I looked fit. My eye was clear and my double chin had disappeared. Also, I had conquered my fight with my appetite. I had won out. I was satisfied with the smaller quantities of food and I felt better than I had in twenty years--stronger, fitter--and was better, mentally and physically. After that it was a cinch. I kept along, eating everything on the bill-of-fare, but in small quantities. I didn't vary my diet a bit, except for the eggs at breakfast. If I wanted pie I ate a small piece. If I wanted ice cream I ate a small dish. If I wanted pudding I ate some of that. I ate fat meat and lean meat and spaghetti, and everything else interdicted by the reduction dietists--only in small quantities! And I kept on getting smaller and smaller.

The fat came off from everywhere. I had been incased with it apparently. My waist decreased seven inches. A big layer of fat came off my chest and abdomen. My legs and arms grew smaller but harder. Even my fingers grew smaller. My excess of chin evaporated. And at the end of the fifth month I had taken off fifty-five pounds.  I weighed then one hundred and ninety-five pounds, which is what I weigh today.

Every person, I take it, has a normal weight; and if that person gives his body a chance, and ill health does not intervene, the body will find that normal and stay there.  I take it that my normal weight, on account of my big frame and bones, is about one hundred and ninety-five pounds, at the age of forty-three.  At any rate, it has stayed at a hundred and ninety-five since the first of last July, and in that time I have loafed for two months and ridden on Pullman cars for two other months, and have not taken any exercise to speak of; but I have maintained my schedule of eating and I have not taken any alcohol.  I figure I can stay where I am indefinitely on that program--and that is my program indefinitely.

There are certain economic phases of a campaign of this kind that should be mentioned.  It is expensive.  Not one item of clothing, save my hat, socks and shoes, which fitted me last January is of the slightest use to me now.  I didn't get to cutting down clothes until I was sure I would stick.  Since that time the tailors have had a picnic at my expense.  My shirts were too big.  Instead of wearing a seventeen-and-three-quarters collar, I now wear a sixteen-and-three-quarters. My waist is seven inches smaller. I even had to have a seal ring I wear cut down so it would not slip off my finger. While in the transition stage I looked like a scarecrow. My clothes hung on me like bags.

Since I have had my clothes re-made and new ones constructed I am an object of continual comment among my friends. They all marvel at my changed appearance. They are all solicitous about my health. They do not see how a man can take off more than fifty pounds and not hurt himself. I do not see how he can keep it on and not kill himself. They tell me I look like a boy--and I feel like one. I'm as active as I was twenty years ago. When I was in the mountains this summer, at an altitude of seventy-five hundred feet, I could climb slopes with no exhaustion that I couldn't have gone fifteen feet up the year before. My mind is clearer; my body is better. I figure I have added a good many years to my life.

And all this time I have had everything I wanted to eat, but not all I wanted to eat until I got myself read-justed to the new system. I missed the alcohol at first, but that is all over now.  It was a part of the game and I used to think a necessary part.  I have cured myself of that delusion.  If there is a thing on earth the matter with me the ablest doctors in this country can't find out what it is.  I am a rejuvenated, reconstructed person, no longer fat, aged forty-three--and the White Man's Hope!

As to the exercise end of it, there wasn't any exercise end.  It happened that I met a man last March, when I was in the first throes of this campaign, who had made some study of the human body.  I liked him because he was modest about what he knew, and not a faddist. We talked about exercise.  He told me one thing that stuck.  He said: "Walk a little every day.  If you have half an hour walk a mile.  If you have an hour walk two miles.  Don't try to see how many miles you can walk in the half-hour or the hour, but take your time.  Look at things as you go along.  Be leisurely about it.  When a man goes out for a walk and walks as hard as he can or does anything else in the shape of exercise as hard as he can he is subjecting himself to just as much nerve strain as he can subject himself to in any other way.  Be calm about your walking, or whatever else you do."

Formerly it had been my custom to plug out after breakfast and gallop three or four miles as hard as I could and then go to work. I cut that out. I walked an easy, leisurely mile or two miles, looking at the trees and flowers and watching the people and looking into shop windows, and I got a lot of good out of it. Then it grew hot, and I cut my walking to half a mile or so down to my office in the morning and back at night. Occasionally, after dinner, I would walk a couple of miles. This summer I went fishing and tramped about some, but not much. In reality, I had no scheme of exercise, and I took little. I didn't need it. I didn't have masses of food and drink in me to be burned up. I was normal.

As I said, I suppose all this is absurdly unscientific-- and I don't give a hoot if it is. It worked for me. I don't know whether it will work for any other person on this earth. Nor do I care. If you want to try it on, provided you are fat, here are the specifications: I assume it is an axiom that we all eat too much. I know I did--about sixty per cent too much. Still, I guarantee nothing. I make no claims. I have set down the facts; and the only warning, advice or admonition I have to give is that any person who makes up his mind to try this method and thinks he isn't in for the hardest struggle of his life would do well not to try. This isn't a frolic.  It's a fight.

### The Codes Of Hammurabi And Moses
### W. W. Davies

QTY

The discovery of the Hammurabi Code is one of the greatest achievements of archaeology, and is of paramount interest, not only to the student of the Bible, but also to all those interested in ancient history...

**Religion**     **ISBN:** *1-59462-338-4*      **Pages:132**
*MSRP $12.95*

### The Theory of Moral Sentiments
### Adam Smith

QTY

This work from 1749. contains original theories of conscience amd moral judgment and it is the foundation for systemof morals.

**Philosophy**  **ISBN:** *1-59462-777-0*      **Pages:536**
*MSRP $19.95*

### Jessica's First Prayer
### Hesba Stretton

QTY

In a screened and secluded corner of one of the many railway-bridges which span the streets of London there could be seen a few years ago, from five o'clock every morning until half past eight, a tidily set-out coffee-stall, consisting of a trestle and board, upon which stood two large tin cans, with a small fire of charcoal burning under each so as to keep the coffee boiling during the early hours of the morning when the work-people were thronging into the city on their way to their daily toil...

**Pages:84**

**Childrens**    **ISBN:** *1-59462-373-2*      *MSRP $9.95*

### My Life and Work
### Henry Ford

QTY

Henry Ford revolutionized the world with his implementation of mass production for the Model T automobile. Gain valuable business insight into his life and work with his own auto-biography... "We have only started on our development of our country we have not as yet, with all our talk of wonderful progress, done more than scratch the surface. The progress has been wonderful enough but..."

**Pages:300**

**Biographies/**   **ISBN:** *1-59462-198-5*      *MSRP $21.95*

## The Art of Cross-Examination
## Francis Wellman

QTY

I presume it is the experience of every author, after his first book is published upon an important subject, to be almost overwhelmed with a wealth of ideas and illustrations which could readily have been included in his book, and which to his own mind, at least, seem to make a second edition inevitable. Such certainly was the case with me; and when the first edition had reached its sixth impression in five months, I rejoiced to learn that it seemed to my publishers that the book had met with a sufficiently favorable reception to justify a second and considerably enlarged edition. ..

**Pages:412**

**Reference**   **ISBN: *1-59462-647-2***

*MSRP $19.95*

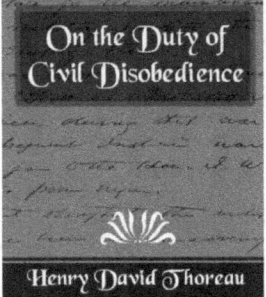

## On the Duty of Civil Disobedience
## Henry David Thoreau

QTY

Thoreau wrote his famous essay, On the Duty of Civil Disobedience, as a protest against an unjust but popular war and the immoral but popular institution of slave-owning. He did more than write—he declined to pay his taxes, and was hauled off to gaol in consequence. Who can say how much this refusal of his hastened the end of the war and of slavery ?

**Law**        **ISBN: *1-59462-747-9***

**Pages:48**

*MSRP $7.45*

## Dream Psychology Psychoanalysis for Beginners
## Sigmund Freud

QTY

Sigmund Freud, born Sigismund Schlomo Freud (May 6, 1856 - September 23, 1939), was a Jewish-Austrian neurologist and psychiatrist who co-founded the psychoanalytic school of psychology. Freud is best known for his theories of the unconscious mind, especially involving the mechanism of repression; his redefinition of sexual desire as mobile and directed towards a wide variety of objects; and his therapeutic techniques, especially his understanding of transference in the therapeutic relationship and the presumed value of dreams as sources of insight into unconscious desires.

**Pages:196**

**Psychology**   **ISBN: *1-59462-905-6***

*MSRP $15.45*

## The Miracle of Right Thought
## Orison Swett Marden

QTY

Believe with all of your heart that you will do what you were made to do. When the mind has once formed the habit of holding cheerful, happy, prosperous pictures, it will not be easy to form the opposite habit. It does not matter how improbable or how far away this realization may see, or how dark the prospects may be, if we visualize them as best we can, as vividly as possible, hold tenaciously to them and vigorously struggle to attain them, they will gradually become actualized, realized in the life. But a desire, a longing without endeavor, a yearning abandoned or held indifferently will vanish without realization.

**Pages:360**

**Self Help**      **ISBN: *1-59462-644-8***

*MSRP $25.45*

QTY

**The Rosicrucian Cosmo-Conception Mystic Christianity** *by Max Heindel*   ISBN: *1-59462-188-8*   **$38.95**
*The Rosicrucian Cosmo-conception is not dogmatic, neither does it appeal to any other authority than the reason of the student. It is: not controversial, but is: sent forth in the, hope that it may help to clear...*   New Age/Religion Pages 646

**Abandonment To Divine Providence** *by Jean-Pierre de Caussade*   ISBN: *1-59462-228-0*   **$25.95**
*"The Rev. Jean Pierre de Caussade was one of the most remarkable spiritual writers of the Society of Jesus in France in the 18th Century. His death took place at Toulouse in 1751. His works have gone through many editions and have been republished...*   Inspirational/Religion Pages 400

**Mental Chemistry** *by Charles Haanel*   ISBN: *1-59462-192-6*   **$23.95**
*Mental Chemistry allows the change of material conditions by combining and appropriately utilizing the power of the mind. Much like applied chemistry creates something new and unique out of careful combinations of chemicals the mastery of mental chemistry...*   New Age Pages 354

**The Letters of Robert Browning and Elizabeth Barret Barrett 1845-1846 vol II**   ISBN: *1-59462-193-4*   **$35.95**
*by Robert Browning and Elizabeth Barrett*   Biographies Pages 596

**Gleanings In Genesis (volume I)** *by Arthur W. Pink*   ISBN: *1-59462-130-6*   **$27.45**
*Appropriately has Genesis been termed "the seed plot of the Bible" for in it we have, in germ form, almost all of the great doctrines which are afterwards fully developed in the books of Scripture which follow...*   Religion/Inspirational Pages 420

**The Master Key** *by L. W. de Laurence*   ISBN: *1-59462-001-6*   **$30.95**
*In no branch of human knowledge has there been a more lively increase of the spirit of research during the past few years than in the study of Psychology, Concentration and Mental Discipline. The requests for authentic lessons in Thought Control, Mental Discipline and...*   New Age/Business Pages 422

**The Lesser Key Of Solomon Goetia** *by L. W. de Laurence*   ISBN: *1-59462-092-X*   **$9.95**
*This translation of the first book of the "Lernegton" which is now for the first time made accessible to students of Talismanic Magic was done, after careful collation and edition, from numerous Ancient Manuscripts in Hebrew, Latin, and French...*   New Age/Occult Pages 92

**Rubaiyat Of Omar Khayyam** *by Edward Fitzgerald*   ISBN:*1-59462-332-5*   **$13.95**
*Edward Fitzgerald, whom the world has already learned, in spite of his own efforts to remain within the shadow of anonymity, to look upon as one of the rarest poets of the century, was born at Bredfield, in Suffolk, on the 31st of March, 1809. He was the third son of John Purcell...*   Music Pages 172

**Ancient Law** *by Henry Maine*   ISBN: *1-59462-128-4*   **$29.95**
*The chief object of the following pages is to indicate some of the earliest ideas of mankind, as they are reflected in Ancient Law, and to point out the relation of those ideas to modern thought.*   Religiom/History Pages 452

**Far-Away Stories** *by William J. Locke*   ISBN: *1-59462-129-2*   **$19.45**
*"Good wine needs no bush, but a collection of mixed vintages does. And this book is just such a collection. Some of the stories I do not want to remain buried for ever in the museum files of dead magazine-numbers an author's not unpardonable vanity..."*   Fiction Pages 272

**Life of David Crockett** *by David Crockett*   ISBN: *1-59462-250-7*   **$27.45**
*"Colonel David Crockett was one of the most remarkable men of the times in which he lived. Born in humble life, but gifted with a strong will, an indomitable courage, and unremitting perseverance...*   Biographies/New Age Pages 424

**Lip-Reading** *by Edward Nitchie*   ISBN: *1-59462-206-X*   **$25.95**
*Edward B. Nitchie, founder of the New York School for the Hard of Hearing, now the Nitchie School of Lip-Reading, Inc, wrote "LIP-READING Principles and Practice". The development and perfecting of this meritorious work on lip-reading was an undertaking...*   How-to Pages 400

**A Handbook of Suggestive Therapeutics, Applied Hypnotism, Psychic Science**   ISBN: *1-59462-214-0*   **$24.95**
*by Henry Munro*   Health/New Age/Health/Self-help Pages 376

**A Doll's House: and Two Other Plays** *by Henrik Ibsen*   ISBN: *1-59462-112-8*   **$19.95**
*Henrik Ibsen created this classic when in revolutionary 1848 Rome. Introducing some striking concepts in playwriting for the realist genre, this play has been studied the world over.*   Fiction/Classics/Plays 308

**The Light of Asia** *by sir Edwin Arnold*   ISBN: *1-59462-204-3*   **$13.95**
*In this poetic masterpiece, Edwin Arnold describes the life and teachings of Buddha. The man who was to become known as Buddha to the world was born as Prince Gautama of India but he rejected the worldly riches and abandoned the reigns of power when...*   Religion/History/Biographies Pages 170

**The Complete Works of Guy de Maupassant** *by Guy de Maupassant*   ISBN: *1-59462-157-8*   **$16.95**
*"For days and days, nights and nights, I had dreamed of that first kiss which was to consecrate our engagement, and I knew not on what spot I should put my lips..."*   Fiction/Classics Pages 240

**The Art of Cross-Examination** *by Francis L. Wellman*   ISBN: *1-59462-309-0*   **$26.95**
*Written by a renowned trial lawyer, Wellman imparts his experience and uses case studies to explain how to use psychology to extract desired information through questioning.*   How-to/Science/Reference Pages 408

**Answered or Unanswered?** *by Louisa Vaughan*   ISBN: *1-59462-248-5*   **$10.95**
*Miracles of Faith in China*   Religion Pages 112

**The Edinburgh Lectures on Mental Science (1909)** *by Thomas*   ISBN: *1-59462-008-3*   **$11.95**
*This book contains the substance of a course of lectures recently given by the writer in the Queen Street Hail, Edinburgh. Its purpose is to indicate the Natural Principles governing the relation between Mental Action and Material Conditions...*   New Age/Psychology Pages 148

**Ayesha** *by H. Rider Haggard*   ISBN: *1-59462-301-5*   **$24.95**
*Verily and indeed it is the unexpected that happens! Probably if there was one person upon the earth from whom the Editor of this, and of a certain previous history, did not expect to hear again...*   Classics Pages 380

**Ayala's Angel** *by Anthony Trollope*   ISBN: *1-59462-352-X*   **$29.95**
*The two girls were both pretty, but Lucy who was twenty-one who supposed to be simple and comparatively unattractive, whereas Ayala was credited, as her Bombwhat romantic name might show, with poetic charm and a taste for romance. Ayala when her father died was nineteen...*   Fiction Pages 484

**The American Commonwealth** *by James Bryce*   ISBN: *1-59462-286-8*   **$34.45**
*An interpretation of American democratic political theory. It examines political mechanics and society from the perspective of Scotsman James Bryce*   Politics Pages 572

**Stories of the Pilgrims** *by Margaret P. Pumphrey*   ISBN: *1-59462-116-2*   **$17.95**
*This book explores pilgrims religious oppression in England as well as their escape to Holland and eventual crossing to America on the Mayflower, and their early days in New England...*   History Pages 268

**QTY**

**The Fasting Cure** *by Sinclair Upton*     ISBN: *1-59462-222-1* **$13.95**
*In the Cosmopolitan Magazine for May, 1910, and in the Contemporary Review (London) for April, 1910, I published an article dealing with my experiences in fasting. I have written a great many magazine articles, but never one which attracted so much attention...* *New Age/Self Help/Health Pages 164*

**Hebrew Astrology** *by Sepharial*     ISBN: *1-59462-308-2* **$13.45**
*In these days of advanced thinking it is a matter of common observation that we have left many of the old landmarks behind and that we are now pressing forward to greater heights and to a wider horizon than that which represented the mind-content of our progenitors...* *Astrology Pages 144*

**Thought Vibration or The Law of Attraction in the Thought World**  ISBN: *1-59462-127-6* **$12.95**
*by William Walker Atkinson*     *Psychology/Religion Pages 144*

**Optimism** *by Helen Keller*     ISBN: *1-59462-108-X* **$15.95**
*Helen Keller was blind, deaf, and mute since 19 months old, yet famously learned how to overcome these handicaps, communicate with the world, and spread her lectures promoting optimism. An inspiring read for everyone...* *Biographies/Inspirational Pages 84*

**Sara Crewe** *by Frances Burnett*     ISBN: *1-59462-360-0* **$9.45**
*In the first place, Miss Minchin lived in London. Her home was a large, dull, tall one, in a large, dull square, where all the houses were alike, and all the sparrows were alike, and where all the door-knockers made the same heavy sound...* *Childrens/Classic Pages 88*

**The Autobiography of Benjamin Franklin** *by Benjamin Franklin*  ISBN: *1-59462-135-7* **$24.95**
*The Autobiography of Benjamin Franklin has probably been more extensively read than any other American historical work, and no other book of its kind has had such ups and downs of fortune. Franklin lived for many years in England, where he was agent...* *Biographies/History Pages 332*

| | |
|---|---|
| **Name** | |
| **Email** | |
| **Telephone** | |
| **Address** | |
| | |
| **City, State ZIP** | |

☐ **Credit Card**   ☐ **Check / Money Order**

| | |
|---|---|
| **Credit Card Number** | |
| **Expiration Date** | |
| **Signature** | |

*Please Mail to:* *Book Jungle*
     *PO Box 2226*
     *Champaign, IL 61825*
*or Fax to:*   *630-214-0564*

## ORDERING INFORMATION
**web***: www.bookjungle.com*
**email***: sales@bookjungle.com*
**fax***: 630-214-0564*
**mail***: Book Jungle  PO Box 2226  Champaign, IL 61825*
**or PayPal** *to sales@bookjungle.com*

*Please contact us for bulk discounts*

## DIRECT-ORDER TERMS

**20% Discount if You Order
Two or More Books**
Free Domestic Shipping!
Accepted: Master Card, Visa,
Discover, American Express